Copyright © 1988 Lark Carrier
Published by Picture Book Studio, Saxonville, MA.
Distributed in Canada by Vanwell Publishing, St. Catharines.
All rights reserved.
Printed in Hong Kong.

Library of Congress Cataloging in Publication Data
Carrier, Lark, 1947–
Do Not Touch.
Summary: Hidden words associated with a child's day at school are revealed
as the reader turns the page.
1. Toy and movable books—specimens. [1. Schools—Fiction. 2. Toy and
movable books] I. Title.
PZ7.C23453Do   1988   [E]   87-32730
ISBN 0-88708-061-8

Ask your bookseller for these other **Picture Book Studio**
books by Lark Carrier:
There Was a Hill . . .
Scout and Cody
A Christmas Promise

Lark Carrier

Do Not Touch

Picture Book Studio

Today's

Surprise

Surprise

What I'm

Hearing

Hearing ring

School Bus

I Never

Knew

Knew **new**

Quite

Bright

Bright
right

Ancient

History

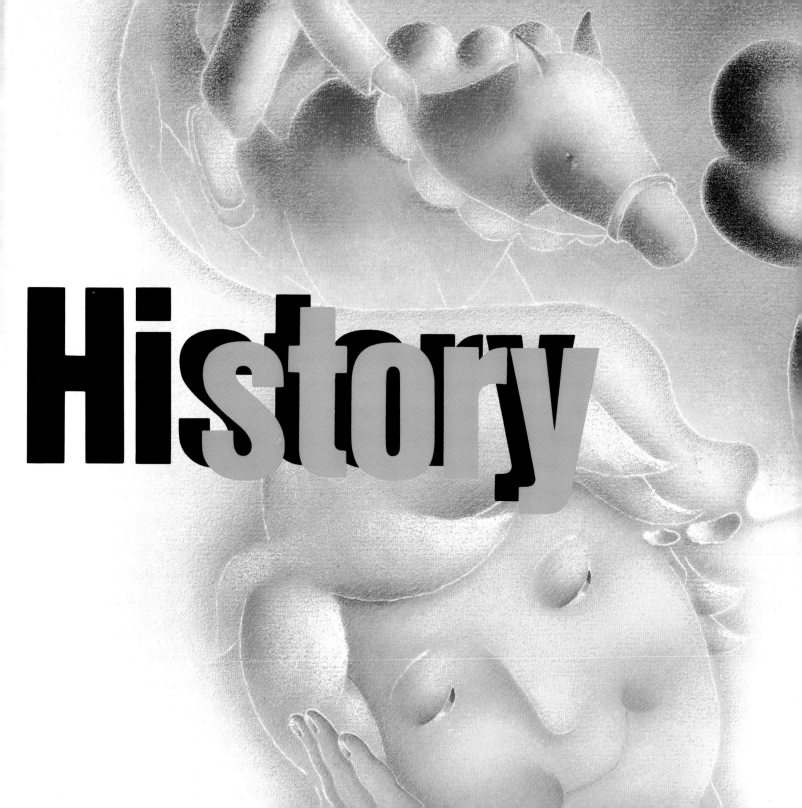

History

Here's

Yours

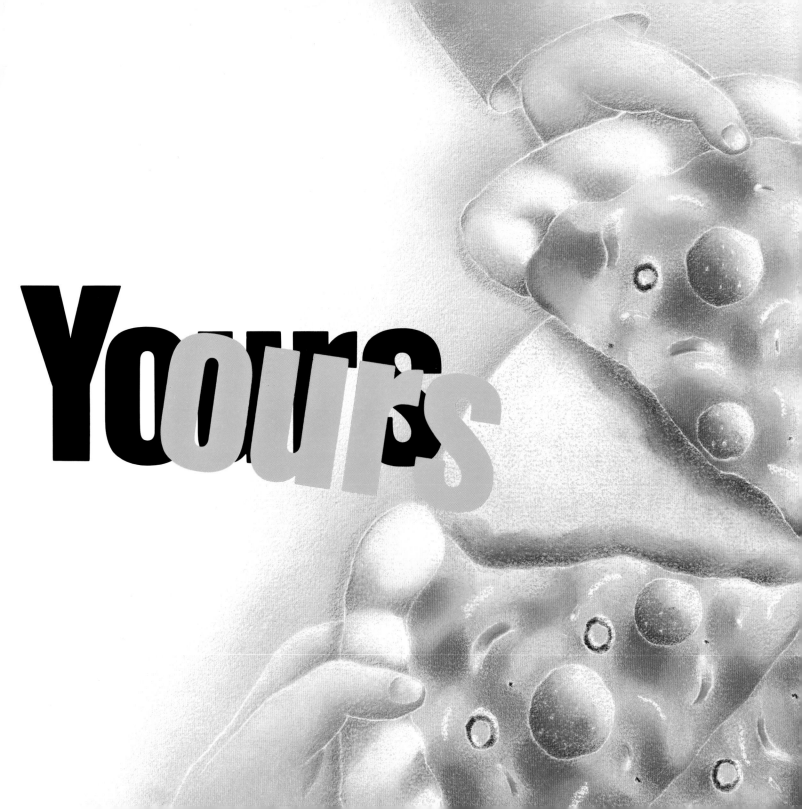

Have a

Treat

Do Not

Touch

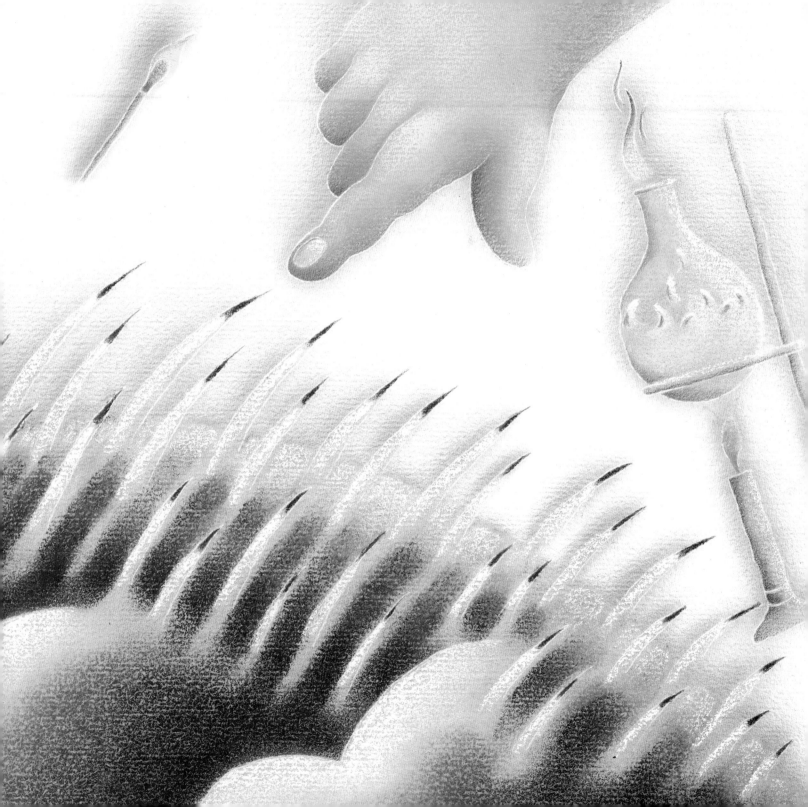

Touch

Take

Flight

From the

Heart

Last

Stop

Stop

With My

Friend

Friend